This book is for Jesse Muse
—J. H. K.

To my wife, Valerie, and my children, Jessica and Keith
—thank you for your patience and support
in completing this project
—F. W.

Rabbit Ears Books is an imprint of Rabbit Ears Productions, Inc.
Published by Simon & Schuster, Inc.
1230 Avenue of the Americas
New York, New York 10020

Manufactured in the United States of America.
10 9 8 7 6 5 4 3 2 1

Library of Congress Cataloging-in-Publication Data

Kunstler, James Howard.
Annie Oakley / written by James Howard Kunstler ; illustrated by Fred Warter.
p.   cm.
Summary: A fictionalized account, told as if by Will Rogers, of the life of the
female sharpshooter who became famous starring in Buffalo Bill Cody's Wild West Show.
ISBN 0-689-80605-1
1. Oakley, Annie, 1860–1926—Juvenile Fiction. [1. Oakley, Annie, 1860–1926—Fiction.
2. Sharpshooters—Fiction. 3. Entertainers—Fiction.] I. Warter, Fred, ill. II. Title.
PZ7.K9496An   1996
[Fic]—dc20   93-19246
CIP
AC

EDITOR'S NOTE: THE AUDIOCASSETTE ACCOMPANYING THIS BOOK IS A THEATRICAL RENDITION
AND DOES NOT EXACTLY MATCH THE TEXT IN THE BOOK.

ANNIE OAKLEY

Written by
James Howard Kunstler

Illustrated by
Fred Warter

RABBIT EARS BOOKS

I fell in love with Annie the first time I saw her ride into the spotlight—an angel in buckskins on a big spotted horse with a star on her wide-brimmed hat, chestnut hair flying out behind, and two six-guns blazing. The cowboy band played "Jubilee!"

May sixteenth, nineteen hundred and one. I'll not forget that day. It gave me my first taste of the show business. I was but twenty-one, a footloose Oklahoma cowpoke at large in New York City, feeling homesick for the short grass and the sage. Buffalo Bill's Wild West show was playing at the old Madison Square Garden, so I paid four bits and went in.

Annie Oakley always opened the show, right from the day Colonel Cody hired her. He figured with so much gunplay and noise on the program, the audience needed a little reassurance right off the bat. So, out he'd send this tiny gal on a great big horse, and she'd commence an astounding display of prowess with the shooting irons. It calmed down women and children to see such a spectacle. I can't vouch the same about the men.

Annie'd circle the arena plugging colored glass balls tossed up by her husband, Frank Butler, who was a crack marksman in his own right, but no match for Little Missie. She'd shoot standing up on her horse's back. She'd hit hens' eggs, champagne corks, Indian head pennies. She'd snuff a candle at fifty paces, sighting backward through a mirror. She'd turn a set of handsprings, grab a shotgun off a table when she landed, and blast two airborne targets with separate barrels, firing straight from the hip. She'd do feats of sharpshooting that would make a whole territory full of Boones and Crocketts turn green with envy. It sure put me and my rope tricks to shame.

Annie was at the very zenith of her glory that night in New York. She'd traveled all over Europe with Colonel Cody's show, met practically all the crowned heads—even took a potshot at one or two of 'em. There was probably no better known lady in all of America. Wherever she and Frank Butler stepped out, crowds would gather. When they walked through the doors at Delmonico's Restaurant, the millionaires stood up and cheered her. Companies wanted to paste her likeness on every possible product: bird shot, cigars, gingersnaps. That pretty little gal had come a long way from her humble beginnings.

She entered the world as Phoebe Ann Moses in the woods of Darke County, Ohio, in 1860—the year before the Civil War broke out. Everybody called her Annie. Western Ohio was still a frontier country, and her people were pioneer farmers.

When Annie was but six years old, her daddy, Jacob Moses, caught the frostbite riding home through a blizzard in an open wagon and died. With him gone, the family fell onto hard times. There were eight children in the Moses clan. Annie was number five. And all but one were girls. The children had to do some part of their daddy's work in order to survive. Annie spent all her days trying to catch wild critters for the supper table, using little traps like Jacob had done.

A couple of years passed and the family barely scraped by. All that time, Jacob's old Pennsylvania rifle hung over the fireplace in the kitchen. None of the other girls dared touch it. One morning when her ma and the rest were out chopping down weeds in the cornfield, Annie snuck off into the woods with Pa's shooting iron. She must have poured a mite too much powder, for the rifle kicked like a mule and broke her nose. But that first shot also brought down a fat partridge. A child doesn't forget an achievement like that.

Well, it finally became clear that they just couldn't make it on the farm, so the family busted apart. The oldest girl married and went off to Cincinnati. Another ran over to Indiana.

Annie found herself farmed out to an orphanage.

By and by, a nice, well-spoken man, name of Wolfe, came along looking to hire some help for his wife. The lucky child who went home with him would live in a fine house and wear shoes and go to school half the day—so he said.

"I'm your gal!" nine-year-old Annie piped right up.

Well now, this Wolfe fellow lived up to his name, and his wife proved to be a snappish breed of she-dog herself, and they cussed and battled from daybreak to moonrise. The fine home he brought Annie to turned out to be a miserable cabin. There wasn't a school around for half a day's ride. And at night, they stuck her in a tiny loft with a straw tick so thin that the bedbugs woke up with backaches. It wasn't a helper they wanted but a slave. Poor Annie endured two years of this bondage before she ran off barefoot for home.

Back in Darke County, she found her mama married to a new husband by the name of Shaw. He was a poor man, but he owned a shotgun and let Annie use it whenever she wanted to—which was every day 'cause she was happiest out hunting critters.

Before long, Annie brought home so much game that she could sell the extras for cash money. That's how shooting turned into a regular business for Annie Moses.

As the years rolled by, there wasn't a boy or a man in Darke County who could outshoot her. And nobody could come close when it came to moving targets, for she was as used to hitting birds on the wing as other folks are to buttering their cornbread.

Annie was fifteen when she heard that the famous marksman, Frank Butler, had issued a hundred-dollar challenge to anyone who could whup him in a shooting match to be held in Cincinnati. Well, she up and bought a train ticket straight to the Queen City of Ohio.

The contest took place in Fairmont Park. Mr. Butler looked splendid in his fancy buckskins, like a prince of the frontier. Imagine what he thought when his opponent turned up in the person of a teenage girl barely five feet tall. And imagine how he felt when the little gal hit twenty-five clay pigeons to his twenty-four. Why, he was so impressed that two years later he swung back through western Ohio and asked Annie to marry him.

"Shoot me for a duck if I won't," she said, and they went right to the preacher.

Together, Mr. and Mrs. Butler hit the road, putting on shooting exhibitions wherever they could roust up a crowd. Annie mostly played Frank's assistant in the show, tossing up targets, trading shots now and then. Before long, though, it became clear that the crowds liked her better. Men sharpshooters were as common as hoop snakes then. But a female with a quick hand and dead eye—now that was a rarity. And worth paying to see. And besides, Annie could just plumb outshoot Frank.

Now Frank Butler was a big-hearted and a practical man, and he loved Annie more than he loved being a show dog. "From now on, you're the star attraction," he told Annie. "But you got to have a stage name all your own so's your fame can stand by itself."

"I'll call myself Oakley," she said. "Annie Oakley."

"It's easy on the eardrums," Frank said. "But where's it come from?"

"I think we passed it yonder whistle-stop," Annie said, pointing out the train window.

Well now, for eight years, Oakley and Butler toured all around the Midwest doing their shooting act in one-night stands. It was better than plowing a furrow, Frank always said, but at times it was a wearisome, unsettled life. They stayed in one hotel room after another, until they all seemed to be the same drabby room. To escape this grind, Oakley and Butler hooked up with the Sells Brothers Circus. It was a big time, big top outfit—clowns, elephants, acrobats, and such. There was more social company traveling with the circus, the meals were better, and Frank and Annie got to stay in one place for a whole week at a time. They might have stuck with it if the Sells brothers had managed to pay a little more regular.

In the winter of 1884, the show came down to New Orleans to work the great cotton expo, and so, as fate would have it, did a newfangled extravaganza called Buffalo Bill Cody's Wild West.

Colonel William F. Cody was one of the most outlandish characters that the frontier ever produced. As a smooth-cheeked boy of fourteen, he rode for the Pony Express. He'd served as a U.S. army scout in several campaigns against the red man, fought bandits up Dakota way, rode with Wild Bill Hickock and General Custer—years before Custer's last stand—and got his nickname, Buffalo Bill, when the Kansas–Pacific Railroad hired him to supply fresh meat to its work gangs. Bill had a hand in practically everything that went on in the territories. He *was* the Wild West, you might say. Then the strangest thing of all happened to Buffalo Bill Cody: He got into the show business.

A fellow wrote some ten-cent books about his exploits. Next thing, someone

hired him to come east and play himself in a theatrical melodrama. Bill was hooked. Playing a frontier hero on stage was a lot safer than getting shot at on the real frontier, and it paid pretty handsome wages, too. Soon he dreamed up the greatest idea of his life: a show that would present the whole pageant of the West—not just in little rosy-hued stage scenes, but in a great big outdoor arena on the grand scale, in all its true wildness and color, complete with real Indians, rough-riding scouts, bloody-minded bad men, live buffalo, moose, elk, and lots of gunplay.

Well, Colonel Cody, as everyone now called him, made his dream come true in short order. The Wild West show was born. It lacked only one thing to make it perfect: a lady heroine as dashing and magnetic as Buffalo Bill himself. And when Colonel Cody saw Annie Oakley walk through the flap of his tent, she must have looked like the heaven-sent answer to his prayers.

Annie Oakley opened the show when it kicked off the 1885 season in Louisville —as she would open every show for the next seventeen years with Mr. Frank Butler assisting. Buffalo Bill's Wild West was an immediate and unqualified success. The show played in baseball parks, race courses, fairgrounds, wherever a grassy sward and an azure sky could let folks pretend that they were out on the Montana range for three hours. Wherever it played, men, women, and children all fell in love with Annie Oakley.

Now in June of that year, Colonel Cody sent one of his most trusted agents away out West to the Standing Rock Reservation to talk to old Chief Sitting Bull, the Sioux medicine man who helped plan the massacre at the Little Bighorn. By now, the government had partly forgiven him for that business on account of General Custer being such a reckless and bloodthirsty fool. Sitting Bull agreed to sign on with the show and instantly became one of its star attractions. He would ride into the arena on an Appaloosa pony and the crowd would boo him until their throats were ragged.

It pretty near broke Annie's heart to witness such a fury of hatred day after day. Finally, she couldn't stand it anymore, and after the performance she went to visit Sitting Bull in his own teepee.

"I guess it ain't my place to say so, Chief, but I wish you wouldn't do that part of the show," Annie told him. "It makes me ashamed for my countrymen."

"Let them bellow at me like buffaloes because I am already a ghost, and maybe they will leave the living Indians alone."

Sitting Bull admired Annie's gumption so much that before long he adopted her as an honorary daughter. They held a big ceremony in the Indian village that was always part of the Wild West encampment. All the warriors who traveled with the show took part: Kills First, Two Bulls, Flying Horse, Sammy Lone-Bear, and the rest. Sitting Bull sang his medicine song, and at the end he gave Annie her new name in Sioux, which was "Little Sure Shot."

Wild West was a hit everywhere in the States. Mark Twain went to see it three times the summer that it played New York, and President Cleveland danced with Annie after the show at the cowboys' ball.

Next, the show went on to even bigger triumphs in England. The whole troupe sailed across the Atlantic on a steamship—cowboys, Indians, horses, even Colonel Cody's pet moose—and then set up camp at the Earl's Court grounds in London. Lords and ladies flocked to see the new arrivals.

One day, the royal box was so crammed full of crowned heads that it looked like a deck of cards. Besides old Queen Victoria there was the king of Greece, the king of Denmark, the crown prince of Sweden, and a whole herd of dukes and duchesses, including Michael, the grand duke of Russia, who was supposedly in England shopping for a wife. Those royals only married other royals, even if they couldn't speak the same lingo.

Well, sir, this Grand Duke Michael fancied himself a sportsman, and he sent a note requesting a shooting match with Annie so's he could show off before all of society. Annie was all for it, knowing she could best any man, on royal or free soil.

Poor Colonel Cody was all in a fret about the etiquette of the thing.

"Little Missie"—he always called her that—"I'm sorry, but you got to let this bird win."

"I don't roll over or play dead for nobody," Annie said.

"But Annie, if you make a fool of him, they'll laugh him out of England," the colonel pleaded. "And who knows but down the road maybe it'll start a war 'twixt Russia and England."

"Boil me for a sea horse if I don't do my level best! Frank, fetch my pistols. We're going after bear!"

Well, of course Annie made short work of Grand Duke Michael. He was a better'n average shot, but better'n average wasn't half good enough to best Annie Oakley. The London newspapers lampooned him without mercy and he skulked back to Russia without a wife. The English royals must not have minded, though, 'cause the prince of Wales became a regular drop-in at Annie's tent each afternoon around teatime, and Queen Victoria herself asked to meet Little Miss Sure Shot.

Annie was so popular in England that she and Frank stuck around even after Colonel Cody and company sailed home. She put on shooting shows on her own, just like in the early days—only now she stayed at castles, not cheap hotels, and hobnobbed with the finest society. She even gave shooting lessons to a princess or two.

She and Frank vamoosed over to Germany. The kaiser there was kin to Queen Victoria, and they'd heard all about Annie. You might say the Germans had an unusual fascination with weapons and in proving how brave they could be. No young German aristocrat felt fully dressed without a dueling scar on his cheek.

At the exhibition in Berlin, the kaiser's own son, Prince Wilhelm, asked Annie

to shoot the ash off a cigar that he held between his teeth. "Well, just a second now, Prince," she protested, but he just wouldn't take no for an answer. Annie just couldn't help thinking: What if this bird sneezes or something?

Well, she did the shot without a hitch, and Prince Willy kept the cigar butt as a souvenir, but all this cavorting with royals was wearing Annie down. She longed to be back in the land of ordinary folks and apple pie, and so she and Frank sailed home.

That was when I first saw her ride into the spotlight in New York City, looking like an angel on horseback.

Well, sir, after I became a headliner with Mr. Ziegfeld's Follies, I went out to see Annie in Dayton, Ohio. She was white-haired and frail by then.

"Hang me up for bear meat, it's Will Rogers!" she said. "I read your column in the papers every week."

I did a few rope tricks for her, and she said they were down right interesting. But why did I have to flap my lips so much? she asked.

"If I was purty, or first-rate with the rope, why, I'd shut pan and sing dumb," I said. "You were a great rifle shot, ma'am, and what you done spoke for itself."

A few weeks later, Annie passed on. But I know that we shall meet again in the sweet by-and-by, because that was her true home. The man upstairs only sent her down here to show the rest of us what it means to be almost perfect.

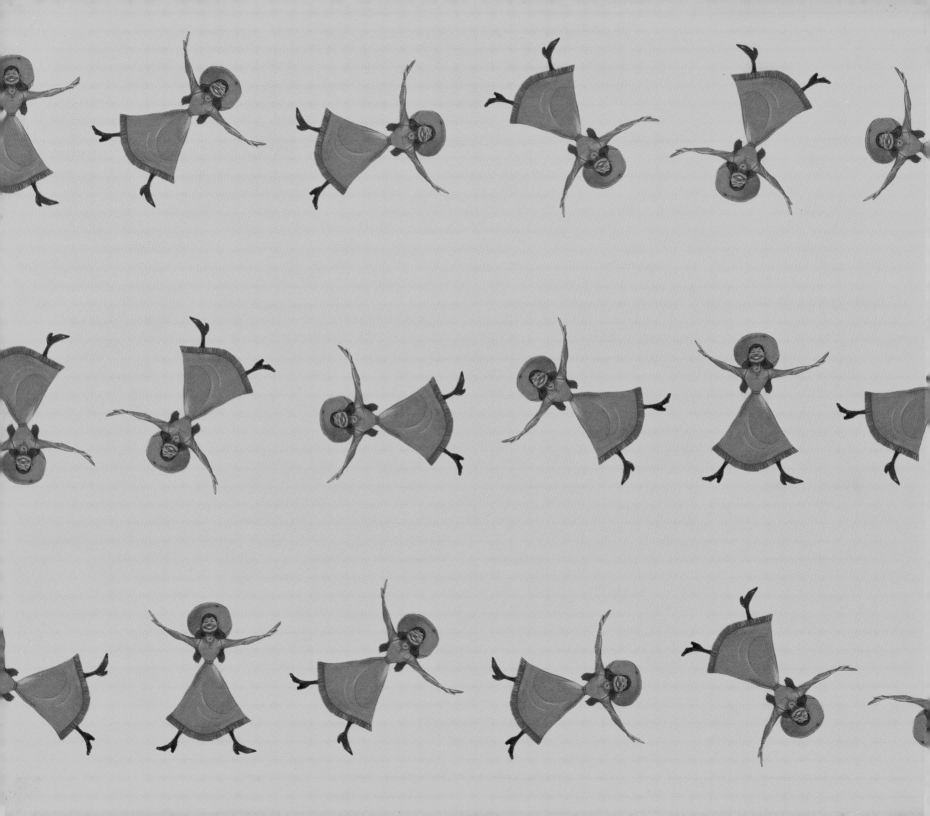